ISBN 0 86112 752 8
© Brimax Books Ltd 1993. All rights reserved.
Published by Brimax Books Ltd, Newmarket CB8 7AU, England 1993.
Reprinted 1995.
Printed in Hong Kong.

AESOP'S FABLES

Illustrated by ERIC KINCAID

Brimax • Newmarket • England

INTRODUCTION

Aesop first told his fables to the Ancient Greeks. Little did he know
that even now, centuries later his fables would still be popular with
both young and old.
Aesop did not actually write the fables down himself. Others who
heard the fables realised how interesting people found them and
wrote them down for him. The original fables were re-discovered
during the last century and were illustrated for Victorian children to
enjoy.
This edition has been beautifully illustrated by Eric Kincaid and is
sure to delight the child of today.

CONTENTS

THE FOX AND THE GRAPES

The fox came padding across the fields in the golden sunlight. His pointed ears were alert. He sniffed the air for any sign of danger. He was a fox and all men were against him.

At the edge of a vineyard he stopped. Thousands of tangled vines crept over high wooden frames. Hanging from the vines were great bunches of juicy grapes.

"I'll steal some before the owner comes," the fox decided.

He reached up and snapped at the nearest grapes. The bunch was too far above his head. Snarling with rage he backed off and leapt into the air, snapping with his great jaws.

He missed! Howling with rage, the fox tried again. For over an hour he ran and jumped, ran and jumped. He could not reach any of the grapes.

At last he gave up and slunk away. "I didn't want those grapes at all, really," he muttered. "They were sour and useless!"

MORAL: *Sometimes when we cannot get what we want, we pretend that we did not want it at all really.*

JUPITER AND THE MONKEY

There was great excitement among the animals. The god Jupiter was going to give a prize to the animal who had the most beautiful baby.

From all over the jungle they gathered. They came from the hills and the valleys, the plains and the rivers. They all brought their babies with them to be judged.

With a great fanfare of trumpets, the god Jupiter arrived among them, coming down from the skies. He walked among the hundreds of animals, looking at each baby very carefully before making up his mind.

One of the animals was a monkey, clutching her child. Jupiter stopped and laughed when he saw the flat-nosed, hairless little baby.

"What on earth are you doing here?" he roared. "You have no chance of winning the prize. I have never seen such an odd-looking little creature in my life!"

The great god passed on. The monkey held her child close to her.

"I don't care what Jupiter or anyone else thinks," she whispered. "To me you are the most beautiful baby in the world."

MORAL: *Beauty is in the eye of the beholder.*

THE NORTH WIND AND THE SUN

The North Wind and the Sun met far above the earth and had a great argument.

"I am stronger than you!" roared the North Wind.

"Oh no, you're not!" smiled the Sun happily.

For weeks their argument raged. Neither the Sun nor the North Wind would give way. They became so wrapped up in their dispute that they ignored their jobs. The North Wind did not blow, and the Sun would not shine.

In the end they decided that they must settle their argument once and for all, before something dreadful happened to the weather on earth.

In the end they agreed that the first of them to separate a certain traveller from his cloak could consider himself the stronger of the two.

The North Wind tried first. He leapt upon the poor traveller, roaring and blowing. He tried his hardest to tear the cloak from the man's body. He failed. All that he did was to make the windswept man hug his cloak closer to him for protection.

"It's impossible," groaned the North Wind, retiring and leaving the traveller to continue on his way. "If I can't separate that man from his cloak with all my strength, I'm sure that you won't be able to, Sun."

The Sun did not answer the surly North Wind. He merely carried on smiling. He smiled down on the traveller below him. His smile began to make the traveller feel warm. Before long, the man stopped hugging his cloak to him and let it fall open. The Sun's smile grew warmer and warmer. The traveller threw his cloak back behind him, so that it hung from his shoulders. Still the Sun smiled. The earth grew warmer and warmer. Everything began to wilt and droop in the enormous heat. In the end, the traveller knew that he did not need his cloak at all. He took it off and trailed it in the dust behind him.

The Sun turned to the North Wind. He still said nothing, but his smile grew even wider.

MORAL: *It is sometimes possible to gain by persuasion what cannot be gained by force.*

THE PEACOCK AND THE CRANE

Once there was a peacock who was very proud and vain. He boasted to everyone about his beautiful feathers. If it rained, he would stand looking at his reflection in puddles.

"Just look at my tail!" he would crow. "Look at the colours of my feathers. I am so beautiful! I must be the most beautiful bird in the world!"

At this he would open his tail like a great fan and stand waiting for someone to come along and admire him.

The other birds became annoyed at the boasts of the proud peacock and tried to think of a way of taking him down a peg or two. It was the great bird called the crane who had an idea.

"Leave it to me," he told the others. "I'll make that vain peacock look foolish."

One morning the crane strolled past the peacock. As usual the peacock was preening his feathers.

"Am I not beautiful!" he cried. "You are so plain and dull, Crane. Why don't you try to look a little smarter?"

"Your feathers may be more beautiful than mine," said the crane calmly. "But I notice that you cannot fly. Your beautiful feathers are not strong enough to lift you from the ground. I may be dull, but my wings can carry me into the sky!"

MORAL: *We may lose in one way, but gain in another.*

17

THE OX AND THE FROGS

A family of frogs lived happily in the rushes of a pool. The two little frogs in the family spent hours every day playing happily at the side of this pool. They made friends with all the other occupants of the pool and all the animals who came to drink the water there.

One day, however, a dreadful accident took place. A great ox came lumbering down to the water's edge to drink. This beast was so big that he did not notice the two little frogs. As he made his way to the edge of the pool, he trod on one of them and squashed him flat.

Sadly the remaining little frog went home and reported to his mother what had happened at the water's edge.

"A great big creature trod on my brother and killed him," he wailed.

"How big was this animal?" demanded his mother. She puffed out her cheeks and her sides. "Was he as big as this?" she asked.

"Oh, much, much bigger than that," replied the little frog.

The frog's mother puffed and puffed and puffed. She made herself as big and as round as a very fat pumpkin.

"Was he as big as . . . ." she began – but then she burst.

MORAL: *There are some things which it is better not to know.*

18

THE WOLF AND THE HORSE

A wolf was slinking across the fields, looking for mischief. He passed by a field of oats, waving in the soft breeze. The wolf stopped hopefully, sniffing around for the scent of some small creature he could hunt down and eat. There was no sign of any living thing, however, so the disappointed wolf went on his way across the fields.

Some time later, the wolf met a horse. The hair on the wolf's back rose and he snarled to himself. But he said nothing to annoy the horse. The wolf hated all other creatures, but he was not going to fall out with one as big and as strong as the horse.

Instead the crafty wolf tried to think of some way of making himself agreeable to the horse. Out of the corner of his eye he saw the field of oats waving in the wind.

"Look at that fine field of oats over there," he said. "I saw you coming and I know horses like eating oats, so I left them all for you. Wasn't that kind of me?"

"You don't fool me," grunted the horse, not at all impressed. "I know that wolves don't eat oats. If you did they would all be gone by now."

MORAL: *There is no virtue in giving someone something we do not want ourselves.*

THE HARE AND THE TORTOISE

The hare was a very fast runner, like most of his kind. He was always teasing the tortoise.

"You are so very slow," he would sigh as the tortoise ambled by. "I wouldn't be surprised if you were the slowest creature in the world. I don't suppose you even known how to hurry."

"Oh, I think I could move fast enough if I had to," said the tortoise happily, inching his way along.

The hare laughed. "What a funny idea," he jeered. "Why, I suppose you even think you could beat me in a race."

The tortoise stopped and thought. "Yes, I do," he said finally.

"Very well," the hare told him indignantly. "If you want to make a fool of yourself, we'll have a race."

The proposed contest aroused a great deal of interest among all the animals. On the day of the race they turned out in great numbers to see the fox start the two creatures off over the course he had arranged.

The hare set off at such a great pace that soon he had left the tortoise far behind and out of sight. Before long the winning post was looming up before the running hare. Suddenly an idea came to the animal and he skidded to a halt.

"I'll really rub it in," he said to himself. "I'll wait here until that poor tortoise comes into sight and then he can see me skip past the winning post."

With that idea in mind, the hare sat down under a tree for the time it would take for the tortoise to appear. It was a very hot day. Before long the hare had fallen asleep.

Meanwhile, the slow old tortoise had been plodding on doggedly. He passed the tree and the sleeping hare. Then he passed the winning post. The cheers of the watching animals woke the hare. To his amazement he saw that he had lost.

MORAL: *Slow and steady can win the race.*

THE SPENDTHRIFT AND THE SWALLOW

A man came into a fortune. Instead of putting some by in a safe place for his old age, he set out to spend all his money as quickly as he could. He became a spendthrift, someone who must buy everything he sees.

Before long, the foolish man had nothing left but the clothes he stood up in. He did not have a single coin left of all his fortune. Still he was not worried. He believed that the future would take care of itself. Somehow or other he would be all right.

One day, as he was walking along a country road on a fine spring morning, he felt happy and lazy. The sun was shining and the air was warm.

As he ambled along the road without a care in the world, he glanced up into the sky. Swooping between the white clouds was a solitary bird.

"I do believe that's a swallow!" exclaimed the man with delight. "They only fly here when summer is on the way. There must be many other swallows coming. That means that summer is almost here."

The man thought that he had solved his problems. If summer was coming, he would not need his coat. He could sell his coat and buy food with the money.

He did just that, selling his fine coat to the first person he met on the road.

But almost at once, things began to go wrong. The spring weather turned very cold, killing many birds and wild animals. The shivering man came across the swallow's frozen body on the ground.

"Because of you I sold my coat," he wailed. "Now I am freezing!"

MORAL: *One swallow does not make a summer.*

THE LARK AND THE FARMER

When it was time to build her nest the lark did so in a field of corn, not in a tree like most other birds. She laid her eggs in this nest and watched them hatch out into young birds. Life was very good among the waving corn.

Then one day, the farmer who owned the field came walking across to look at it.

"Hmm, very nice," he said. "This corn is just about ready to harvest. I think I'll have a word with my neighbours and ask them to help me gather it in."

At this the young larks were very frightened and set up a great twittering.

"Quick, Mother, we must move before our nest is destroyed!"

Their mother was too wise to be worried by such talk.

"Hush, my darlings," she soothed. "There is nothing to worry about yet. A man who talks about going to his neighbours for help can be in no great hurry. We can wait a little longer."

A few days later, when the corn was so ripe it was falling to the ground, the farmer walked across the field again.

"I must hire some men and gather in this corn at once," he said.

"Come, my children," sighed the mother lark. "Now the farmer is relying upon himself, not others. It is time for us to move."

MORAL: *If we really want something done, it is best to do it ourselves.*

THE STAG AT THE POOL

A fine stag went to the pool to drink. When he had drunk deeply of the water there, he stood and gazed at his own reflection. His great twisted horns called antlers looked magnificent.

"I really do have a very fine pair of antlers," the stag said proudly. "They are very handsome indeed."

He turned away. As he did so he caught a glimpse of his legs reflected in the pool. Some of his feeling of pride left him.

"What a pity my legs are not as fine as my antlers," he said sadly. "It is very true that my legs are far too weak and thin. I wish I could do something to improve them."

A lion who had been creeping up on the stag suddenly leapt out at him. At once the stag fled. The ground ahead was open and free from trees. The stag's legs served him well. Soon he drew ahead of the lion. He dashed into a forest. Unfortunately his fine antlers became tangled in the branches of a tree, forcing the stag to come to a halt until the lion caught up with him.

"What a fool I was!" cried the stag as the lion leapt upon him. "The legs I despised have served me well, while the antlers of which I was so proud have let me down."

MORAL: *What is worth most is often valued least.*

THE MOUSE AND THE BULL

When it happened, it surprised everyone. A cheeky little mouse went up to a bull as the great animal was grazing. Suddenly the mouse darted forward and bit the great bull on the nose.

The bull roared with surprise and fury. The mouse turned and fled. Lowering his horns the bull charged after the tiny creature.

Just when it looked as if the bull would catch up with the mouse and toss it high into the air, the tiny animal reached its hole in a wall and scuttled in to safety.

The bull snorted and pawed the ground outside the hole, daring the mouse to come out and face him. The mouse laughed at him.

This was too much! The bull backed off and then charged at the wall, butting it with his head. He repeated this several times. The strong wall did not even shake. The bull realised that his head was now very sore. He felt dizzy and sank to his knees.

This was just what the mouse had been waiting for. As the exhausted bull sprawled on the ground, his head only a short distance from the hole, the mouse darted out and bit him on the nose again!

This time the bull's angry roar could be heard all over the fields. He rose to his feet and tried to trample on the mouse. The big animal was far too slow. The mouse was already back in his hole.

The bull bellowed and stamped his feet until the ground shook. There was nothing else he could do.

Presently a little voice squeaked from the safety of the wall.

"You big strong fellows don't win all the time, you know!"

MORAL: *Size and strength is not always enough.*

THE BIRDS, THE BEASTS AND THE BAT

The birds and beasts were at war. Their battles were fierce and frequent. Sometimes the birds won, swooping down out of the sun and attacking the animals. Sometimes the beasts won, creeping up on the birds as they searched for food on the ground, and leaping on them.

But there was one creature who was always on the winning side. He never lost, because he kept on changing sides. He would fight for the birds until they looked like losing, and then change sides. For a time he would fight for the animals, and then if the birds gained the upper hand, he would change back and join *them*.

This creature was the bat. He thought he was a very clever fellow, always being on the winning side.

In the end the war ended. The birds and the beasts agreed to live in peace for ever.

"Now I shall get my reward," the bat told himself. "Everyone will think I'm a fine fellow. After all, *I* was never on the losing side. I helped both sides. In fact, the birds and the beasts may make me their king!"

It did not work out like that at all. Neither the birds nor the beasts would have anything to do with him!

"You are a traitor!" they told the amazed bat. "You are loyal to no one. You only serve yourself. You let down both sides in the war. We want nothing more to do with you."

From that day to this the bat was an outcast, ignored by both the birds and the beasts.

MORAL: *People are expected to be loyal and to stick by their friends.*

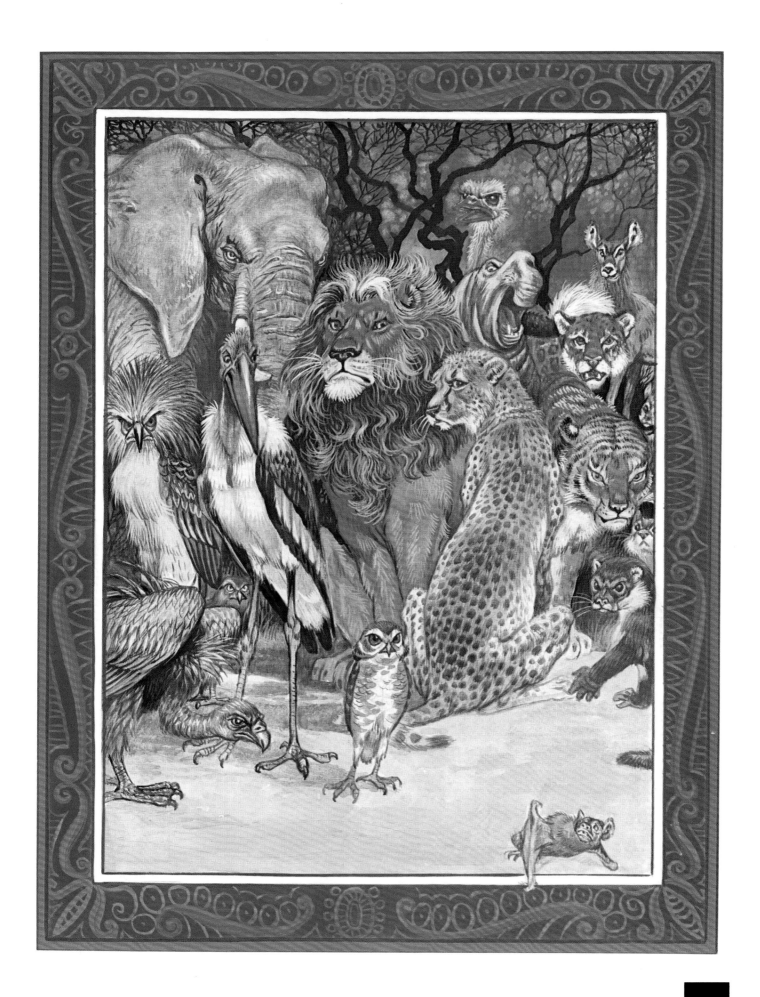

THE FOX AND THE CROW

A hungry fox was prowling along looking in vain for food. It had been a long day and he was very hungry.

"What I would like more than anything else in the world," he said longingly to himself, "would be a nice piece of cheese."

Just as the thought passed through his head, the fox glanced up at the branches of a tree he was passing. To his amazement he saw a black crow sitting in the tree. In her beak was a piece of cheese. The fox licked his lips greedily. Somehow or other he had to get that cheese from the bird.

"Oh, Crow," he said admiringly, as if butter would not melt in his mouth, "what a beautiful bird you are. Your feathers are so soft and black, your beak so beautifully curved. If only – "

The fox stopped and shook his head doubtfully. The crow looked down, wondering what the fox was going to say next.

"If only," went on the fox, "your voice was as beautiful as your appearance, you would be a queen among birds."

Greatly flattered, the bird opened her beak and cawed loudly to show that she could sing. As she did so, the piece of cheese fell to the ground. The fox picked the cheese up and ran off with it.

MORAL: *Beware of flattery, it may not be meant.*

THE LION AND THE MOUSE

The lion was proud and strong, and king of the jungle. One day while he was sleeping, a tiny mouse ran over his face. The great lion awoke with a snarl. He caught the mouse with one mighty paw and raised the other to squash the tiny creature who had annoyed him.

"Oh, please, mighty lion!" squeaked the mouse, "please do not kill me. Let me go, I beg you. If you do, one day I may be able to help you in some way."

This greatly amused the lion. The thought that such a small and frightened creature as a mouse might be able to help the king of the jungle was so funny that he did not have the heart to kill the mouse.

"Go away," he growled.

A few days later, a party of hunters came into the jungle. They decided to try to capture the lion. They climbed two trees, one on either side of the path, and held a net over the path.

Later in the day the lion came loping along the path. At once the hunters dropped their net on the great beast. The lion roared and fought mightily, but he could not escape from the net.

The hunters went off to eat, leaving the lion trapped in the net, unable to move. The lion roared for help, but the only creature in the jungle who dared come near was the tiny mouse.

"Oh, it's you," groaned the lion. "There's nothing you can do to help me. You're too small."

"I may be small," said the mouse, "but I have sharp teeth and I owe you a good turn!"

Then the mouse began to nibble at the net. Before long he had made a hole big enough to allow the lion to crawl through and make his escape into the jungle.

MORAL: *Sometimes the weak are able to help the strong.*

THE BEE-KEEPER AND THE BEES

There was once a bee-keeper who looked after a number of bee-hives together. We call such a collection of hives an apiary.

The bee-keeper kept his bees for their honey, but like all good bee-keepers he never took all the honey from the hives, but always left some for the bees.

One day a thief waited until the bee-keeper had gone off for his lunch and all the bees were out of the hives looking for pollen, from which they could make honey.

The thief was very greedy. He broke up the hives and took every scrap of honey that he could find. Then he ran off with it.

When the bee-keeper came back he saw what had happened. He was very upset.

"My poor bees!" he cried. "What will they do when they see their hives broken and all their honey stolen? I must try to put things right before they get back."

He set out to do this. He was just picking up the pieces of one of the broken hives when a swarm of bees returned. They saw all the damage and the broken honeycombs which had once held their honey. They also saw the bee-keeper standing over their ruined home. They thought that he must have destroyed it.

BZZZZZZZZ! They were very angry. They attacked the poor bee-keeper and stung him again and again.

"It's not fair!" he shouted. "You let the man who stole your honey go free but you sting your friend and helper!"

MORAL: *Things are not always what they seem.*

THE OAK AND THE REEDS

An oak tree grew by the river. It was such a big tree and so proud of its size and strength.

"I am the biggest and strongest of all trees," he would cry loudly. "No one can bother me!"

Quite close to the oak tree, by the river bank, grew a clump of reeds. These reeds were quiet and shy, whispering softly as they swayed in the breeze.

One day a fierce wind blew across the land. It howled and roared. It tore the branches from trees and sent the roofs of houses spinning off.

The oak tree stood and faced the wind, daring it to do its worst. It had always been stronger than any wind.

But that day the wind was stronger than the oak. It tore the tree up by the roots and sent it crashing to the ground. The stricken oak fell among the clump of reeds. The reeds were still swaying from side to side, they did not seem bothered by the wind.

"I don't understand it," sobbed the oak. "How can someone as frail and slender as a reed escape the anger of the wind, while a strong tree has been torn up by the roots!"

"You were too stubborn," whispered the reeds. "You stood and fought the wind, although it was stronger than you were. We reeds knew that we were weak and frail, so we bent before the wind and let it pass harmlessly over our heads."

MORAL: *Sometimes in order to survive it is better to give way.*

A WOLF IN SHEEP'S CLOTHING

"There are dozens of sheep in that flock down there," said a wicked old wolf to himself, gazing down at a field. "How can I get close to them so that I can kill and eat some?"

Then he had an idea. He found an old sheepskin and wrapped himself up in it, so that he looked like a sheep. Then he walked down to the field and joined the flock of sheep grazing there.

The sheep thought that the wolf was one of them, so they paid no attention to him as he moved among them. Not even the shepherd noticed who the wolf really was.

The wolf decided that it would be best to wait until dark before he fell on the fattest sheep and ate it. By that time the shepherd would have gone home.

When the sun went down behind the distant hills, the shepherd drove his sheep and the wolf in the old sheepskin into the pen which gave them shelter at night. Then he went off to his cottage to sleep.

The wolf had just decided which sheep he was going to leap upon, when suddenly the door of the pen was thrown open. A farmer stood in the doorway.

"We want some fresh meat at the farmhouse," he said. "One of you sheep will do. Yes, you over there! You look a big fellow."

With that, the farmer lifted his axe and brought it crashing down on the wolf, thinking that he was a sheep.

MORAL: *Sometimes we can be too clever for our own good.*

42

THE GRASSHOPPER AND THE ANTS

All through the long summer days, the ants had worked away gathering food to store for the winter days when snow lay deep on the ground.

As they gathered their food and put it in their store-house the idle grasshopper looked at them and laughed.

"Poor fools!" he called. "Why do you work when the sun is high in the sky? This is a time for singing and playing."

The ants paid no attention to him. They went on working hard, collecting enough food to see them through the long winter days and nights. As they did so the grasshopper lay in the sun, singing happily.

But in the end the summer went away. Winter ruled in the land, covering everything with snow and ice. There was no food to be seen anywhere. The grasshopper, who had stored no food in the summer months, was starving. He limped along to the store-house where the ants had stored their food.

"What do you want?" asked the ants, as they carried on sweeping, tidying and sorting. The ants were always busy.

"I am very hungry," begged the grasshopper. "Please give me some of the food you have saved, or I will starve to death."

"You should have thought of that in the summer when you were busy with your playing and singing," said the ants. "If you spent the summer singing, then maybe you should spend the winter dancing, and not bother about eating at all."

The ants would not give the grasshopper a single scrap of their food, and he went away sad and hungry.

MORAL: *We should always make plans for the future.*

THE FISHERMAN AND THE SPRAT

It had been a bad day for the poor fisherman. He had sailed his small craft out into the wide sea at dawn. All day he had been casting his nets into the water and then drawing them out again. Each time he did so, the nets remained empty.

"Can there be a single fish left in the sea, I wonder?" the man grumbled. "It certainly doesn't seem so."

He was about to give up and sail sadly back to port, when he drew in his nets for the last time. Something was wriggling in the bottom of one of the nets. His heart leaping, the fisherman hurried forward to see what he had caught. To his disgust he saw that he had caught one small sprat, the tiniest of fish.

This particular sprat was so small that it fitted easily into the palm of the fisherman's hand.

"Please let me go," begged the small fish. "You can see for yourself that I am no use to you as I am. But if you throw me back into the water, I shall grow up into a fine big fish. Then you can catch me again in a year's time, when I will make a meal."

"No way," said the man. "If I let you go you would vanish!"

MORAL: *A fish in the hand is worth two in the sea.*

THE BOY AND THE WOLF

The wolf was prowling over the fields looking for food. A boy saw the wolf coming and turned to flee. He realised that the wolf would catch up with him in a few seconds, so instead he tried to hide in some long grass.

The wolf found the boy's hiding place almost at once. He came loping over to the child, his teeth bared.

"Please, Mr Wolf, do not eat me," begged the boy, trembling with fear.

The wolf hesitated. He had intended to kill and eat the boy, but he had to admit that he had already caught plenty of small animals that day, and he was not really very hungry. He decided instead to have some sport with the terrified child.

"Very well," he said, licking his lips. "I will spare your life, if you tell me three things which are so true that I cannot possibly disagree with them."

The boy thought rapidly, knowing that his life depended upon his three answers.

"Well," he said slowly, "it's a pity that you saw me."

"That's true," agreed the wolf. "That's one answer."

"And," went on the boy, gaining confidence, "it's a pity I let you see me."

"That's true as well," nodded the wolf. "Very well, you have two out of three. Everything depends upon your third answer."

"Thirdly," said the boy in a rush, "people hate wolves because they attack sheep for no reason at all."

The wolf was silent for a long time. The boy wondered if he had been too bold. But this wolf was fair-minded.

"I suppose that is true from your point of view," he admitted. "Very well, you may go."

MORAL: *A fair-minded person tries to see both sides of an argument.*

THE PIPING FISHERMAN

A fisherman wanted very much to leave the sea and become a musician. He played upon a pipe. He would much rather play the pipe than fish. Every day, however, he had to go down to the sea, throw his nets into the water and hope that they would fill with fish.

One day, he took his pipe with him when he went to work by the side of the rolling ocean.

"Everyone says that I make lovely music with my pipe," he said to himself. "Why don't I play to the fish? My music should attract them and make them come up on to the shore. Then I won't have to bother to throw my nets out."

This is just what he tried to do. The fisherman stood by the sea for hours, playing as well as he could upon his pipe. Not one fish jumped out of the water on to the beach.

In the end, muttering to himself, the disappointed fisherman put his pipe into his pocket and went back to his nets. He threw them into the sea. When he hauled them back in to the shore again they were full of fish.

"Why is it that when I piped not one of you would dance?" he demanded crossly, "but now that I have stopped piping, you are all dancing?"

MORAL: *In order to succeed we have to work, not play.*

51

THE SWAN AND THE CROW

There was once a black crow who wanted to be a white swan. This crow lived in a tree, like all the other crows. He led a perfectly happy life, with a strong nest to live in and good food to eat, but he was not content. He saw the graceful swans beating their way through the air with their strong wings and sailing proudly on rivers, and wanted to be just like one of them.

"I wish my wings and body were white like the swans are," he said to himself. "Why can't I be like a swan? It's just a case of trying hard enough."

So the crow decided to turn himself into a swan. First he went to live by the side of a river, as the swans did, leaving his warm nest in the tree. For weeks he watched the swans as they floated on the water and flew into the sky, trying to remember everything that they did. Then he set out to copy them in every detail.

He taught himself to swim in the flowing water. Each day he scrubbed away at his black feathers, trying to make them white. He ate the same food as the swans.

Nothing worked. The crow's body remained black. The swans' food did not agree with him and he grew thin. The water made his wings weak and bedraggled.

In the end, the crow realised that he was never going to turn himself into a swan. The knowledge disappointed him so much that he flew away from the river and died.

MORAL: *We may change our habits, but we cannot change our nature.*

THE WOLF AND THE GOAT

A cunning wolf saw a goat nibbling grass at the top of a hill.

"What a good dinner you would make," said the wolf to himself, licking his lips hungrily.

He walked forward and gazed longingly up at the goat. He was not nearly as sure-footed as the other animal. There was no way in which he could climb the cliff and fall upon the goat. Somehow he had to persuade the goat to come down to him.

"Good morning, Madam Goat," he called out, putting on his most engaging smile. "Pray take a care. It is so dangerously high on that cliff. I should hate you to come to any harm. I'll tell you what! Why don't you come down here, where the grass is fresh and green. I speak to you as a friend."

The goat was not to be fooled. She looked down at the wolf and shook her head.

"You can't trick me," she called down. "You don't care whether the grass I eat is fresh and green, or dry and brown. All that you want to do is to eat me!"

MORAL: *Look before you leap.*

THE TREES AND THE AXE

A woodman went into a forest. The great trees surrounded him. They were tall and thick and strong. Most of them had been in the forest for hundreds of years.

"I am sorry to disturb you," said the woodman politely, "but I can see that you great trees are the kings of the forest. I have a request to make. I need wood to make a new handle for my axe. I wonder if I could cut down a tree for this purpose. I don't mean one of you, of course, just a small tree somewhere."

The great trees were flattered at being spoken to in this manner and nodded their heads graciously.

"You do not ask for much," they said. "Yes, you may take just one small tree. You may cut down that young sapling over there."

The older trees nodded at a young ash tree which had not had time to grow very tall or thick.

The woodman thanked them for their kindness. He walked over to the ash tree before the older trees could change their minds. With a few swift strokes he cut down the ash tree. Then he sat down and made a fine new handle for his axe from the fallen tree.

As soon as his axe had been repaired in this way, the woodman showed the old trees the real reason for his arrival. Wielding his strong new axe, he cut down every tree that stood in his path. He went right through the forest, hacking and cutting at all the trees he could find, big and small alike.

Before long most of the forest had been cut down. The few surviving trees, who once had welcomed the woodman into their midst, wailed in despair and fear.

"It's our own fault," they cried. "We have brought our deaths upon ourselves. We should not have stood by and let the woodman cut down that first tree. If we had protected that sapling we would have been guarding ourselves."

MORAL: *Unity is strength.*

THE EAGLE AND THE BEETLE

The eagle and a tiny beetle fell out with one another and became deadly enemies.

It happened like this. One day the eagle was chasing a hare across a field. It swooped low over the terrified animal, its great claws extended, its beak ready to strike.

The poor hare ran as fast as it could, screaming for help. The only living thing it could see was the tiny beetle.

"Help me, beetle! Please help me!" cried the hare piteously.

The beetle was small but brave. "Eagle!" he cried in his loudest voice. "I am speaking to you, Eagle! Do not touch that hare. It is under my special protection!"

Of course, the eagle took no notice at all. In fact she hardly noticed the tiny beetle. Suddenly she pounced upon the hare and ate it.

The beetle was very upset about this and decided to avenge the hare.

He made his way to the eagle's nest, high in the cliffs, and waited. Then, every time that the eagle laid an egg, the beetle rolled it out of the nest, so that it fell to the ground below and was smashed.

The beetle destroyed so many eggs in this way that the worried eagle went to the god Jupiter, and asked his advice.

"You may lay your eggs in my lap," said the god. "They will be safe there. The beetle will not dare approach me."

But Jupiter did not know how determined the tiny beetle was. When he started something, the beetle always did his best to finish it. He waited until the eagle had laid a clutch of eggs in the god's lap. Then he rolled a lump of earth into Jupiter's lap.

When the god saw the dirt on his lap he stood up quickly and brushed it off. But he had forgotten that the eagle's eggs were also on his lap. As he stood up, these fell to the ground and were smashed. The beetle had won again!

Since that day, or so it is said, eagles have always made sure that their eggs are laid in a safe place, which is why people hardly ever see them.

MORAL: *Great determination can overcome most odds.*